"Bee My Valentine!"

Miriam Cohen

Pictures by Lillian Hoban

A Young Yearling Book

Published by
Dell Publishing
a division of
Bantam Doubleday Dell Publishing Group, Inc.
666 Fifth Avenue
New York, New York 10103

ISBN: 0-440-40507-6

Reprinted by arrangement with Greenwillow Books, a division of
William Morrow & Company, Inc.

Printed in the United States of America

November 1983

10 9 8

RAI

To Pat Greer,
Osceola Hankins,
and
Mr. Ziskind's First Grade

"Valentine's Day is coming!" said Jim.
He was happy.

He really liked those funny cards
with the bear saying,
"I can't bear it
   if you won't be my Valentine."

"What is Valentine's?" asked Louie.
He was new in first grade.
"It's the day you try to get
the most cards," answered Anna Maria.

"And everybody says, 'You are my sweetheart! You are my sweetheart!'" Willy said.

The teacher said, "On Valentine's Day we send cards to show we like someone. <u>Everybody must send a card to everybody else in first grade</u>. Then nobody will be sad."

"I'm not going to send a card to
Anna Maria,"
Danny whispered to Willy.
And Jim thought, "I'm going to send
two valentines to Paul."

After school, Jim's mother said,
"Why don't you make your
own valentines?"
But Jim remembered how his hearts
always came out fat on one side
and skinny on the other.

And he could never make
those little bees with big eyes—
the ones that said,
"Bee my honey!"

Jim rushed to the ten-cent store.
The other kids were already there.
First they looked at all the candy.
Then they each bought a box of valentines.

Each box was the same and each box had
enough cards in it for everybody in first grade.
"Ooh, this is a cute one! Will you send it
to me, Jim?" asked Anna Maria.
But Jim was thinking which cards
he would send to Paul.

At last it was Valentine's Day.
The teacher called out
the names on the cards.

Jim was hoping he'd get lots of good valentines.
Sara waved a card.
'Look! I got one from Sammy.
It says, 'My two-lips are thine.' "

All the first graders were showing
their valentines and laughing.
They asked each other,
"How many did you get?"

Paul told Jim, "I like the ones you sent me.
I like 'Police be my Valentine.' "
He held up a little policeman on a motorcycle.

Danny yelled, "I have thirteen valentines!"
But some of Danny's cards said,
"To Danny, You are nice, from Danny."
He had sent them to himself.

Jim got twelve valentines.
He kept looking at them.
He loved them all.
"See this one," Anna Maria said to Margaret.
"I kept it for myself
because it was too cute to send."

Some people got a lot of valentines.
Some people didn't get so many.
But George didn't get enough.
He ran and hid in the coatroom
and wouldn't come out.

"Oh, dear," the teacher said. "I'm afraid everyone did not send a valentine to everyone else in first grade. What can we do to make George feel better?"

Everybody tried to think.
It was very quiet except for George.
He was crying in the coatroom.
Anna Maria said, "I'll give him one of
my cards because I have so many."

But George hollered, "I don't want it!"
"I know!" Jim cried.
"We can play music for him."
He took out his harmonica
and began to blow.

Paul went to the music corner
and got the trumpet.
Anna Maria took the kazoo
before anyone else could.
Willy got the drum.

Margaret planged the guitar.
Danny bonged the xylophone,
and Louie whanged the triangle.
Sara put a pretty cloth on her
head and began to dance.

Around the room they went.
George came out slowly.
Sammy gave him the bells to shake.
He knew that was George's favorite.

Willy got the paper crown and
put it on George's head.
"Hey, man, you are the king," he said.

"And look who's here," said the teacher.
Willy's mother was standing in the doorway.
She brought cupcakes shaped
just like pink hearts!

Danny ate his right away and then he pretended
Louie's hat was a big cupcake.
He pretended he was eating it on Louie's head.
Everybody laughed and laughed.

Then it was three o'clock.
They all grabbed their coats
and their cards.
They ran out calling to one another.
"Happy Valentines, Jim."

"Happy Valentines, Paul."
"Happy Valentines, Willy and Sammy and
  Anna Maria and Louie and George and
  Margaret and Sara and *everybody.*
  Happy Valentine's Day!"

ello, I'M
love you
YOUR FRIEND
TINA

GEORGE is
GOOD FROM
Willy

to Sammy
Do you Love Me
Margaret

DANNY.
OU aRE Nice
FROM DANNY

Dear Sara
I like to give you
a Present but I
haven't got
one
Lovie